MOONGOBBLE AND ME
THE WEEPING WEREWOLF

MOONGOBBLE AND ME
THE WEEPING WEREWOLF

Bruce Coville
ILLUSTRATED BY Katherine Coville

SCHOLASTIC INC.

New York   Toronto   London   Auckland   Sydney
Mexico City   New Delhi   Hong Kong   Buenos Aires

No part of this publication may be reproduced, stored in a retrieval system, or transmitted in any form or by any means, electronic, mechanical, photocopying, recording, or otherwise, without written permission of the publisher. For information regarding permission, write to Simon & Schuster Books for Young Readers, Simon & Schuster Children's Publishing Division, 1230 Avenue of the Americas, New York, NY 10020.

ISBN 0-439-79154-5

Text copyright © 2004 by Bruce Coville.
Illustrations copyright © 2004 by Katherine Coville.
All rights reserved. Published by Scholastic Inc.,
557 Broadway, New York, NY 10012, by arrangement
with Simon & Schuster Books for Young Readers,
Simon & Schuster Children's Publishing Division.
SCHOLASTIC and associated logos are trademarks
and/or registered trademarks of Scholastic Inc.

12 11 10 9 8 7 6 5 4 3 2 1   6 7 8 9 10 11/0

Printed in the U.S.A.   40

First Scholastic printing, January 2006

Book design by Lucy Ruth Cummins

The text for this book is set in Historical Fell Type Roman.

The illustrations for this book are rendered in graphite.

For Landon Dietz

CONTENTS

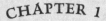

CHAPTER 1

BULLIES

"Hey, Edward!" said Peter Cooper. "Where are you going? Up to see the crazy man?"

"Moongobble isn't crazy," I said, trying not to let Peter make me angry.

"I hear they're never going to let him into the Society of Magicians!" yelled Thomas Baker.

I walked faster, trying to ignore the two boys, as Mother had always told me to do. But I knew that wouldn't work. Peter and Thomas wanted to make me cry, and they wouldn't stop until they did.

I don't know why big kids feel like they have to

pick on smaller kids. Maybe it's not that way other places. But it's sure the way things work in our little town of Pigbone.

"Is Moongobble your mother's boyfriend?" called Peter.

"Does she kiss him?" hooted Thomas.

"Where's your real father?" shouted Peter. "Did he run away because you're so ugly?"

I felt like I was going to explode. I wanted to rush back and hit them. But I had had enough black eyes and bloody noses to know what would happen if I tried.

So I kept walking.

I wished I had Fireball with me.

Fireball is my pet dragon. Well, he's not really a pet; dragons do not believe in being pets. Fireball says he prefers the word "friend." The problem is that Mother thinks trying to keep a dragon—even one that is only four feet long—in a town like Pigbone would cause more trouble than it is worth. So Fireball stays with my other friend, Moongobble the Magician, who lives in the cottage at the top of the hill. He is the "crazy man" Thomas and Peter were talking about. He's not crazy, of course. But he is a little strange.

"Edward is a sissy!" cried Peter.

"Edward is a coward!" cried Thomas.

"Edward doesn't have a father!" they yelled together.

I kept walking, trying not to let them see the tears running down my cheeks. Soon I would be finished with the errand I was doing for Mother. Soon I could climb the hill to Moongobble's cottage. Soon I would be where I really wanted to be.

But when I finally got to the top of the hill, I sensed trouble was there, too. Moongobble's faithful toad, Urk, was squatting on the doorstep. He looked even crankier than usual.

"What's wrong?" I asked.

"We just got a message that Fazwad is coming."

I groaned. "Not already!"

"Yes, already," said Urk.

Fireball came fluttering out of the cottage to land on my shoulder. "I do not like Fazwad," said the little dragon once he had his claws in my shirt. "He's mean, and he's tricky."

I agreed. Fazwad is head of the Society of Magicians. His full title is Fazwad the Mighty. He did not like Moongobble, and did not want to let him join the society. But if Moongobble didn't join, he couldn't do magic in our kingdom. That meant he would either have to give up magic, or move away.

I didn't want Moongobble to leave. He paid me a silver penny every day I helped him. This was good, since Mother and I did not have much money. But the real reason I didn't want him to go was that he was my friend.

The problem was, the first time Fazwad came to test Moongobble's magic, Moongobble flubbed the exam. That had not surprised me. Moongobble always flubs his magic. He has a good heart, but he is not a very good magician. Fortunately, Urk had read the *Society of Magicians Handbook*. He knew that a

4

magician who fails the entry test can still join the society by performing three Mighty Tasks.

Moongobble's first task had been to fetch the Golden Acorns of Alcoona. I had helped with that one, which was how I met Fireball.

Now it was time for another.

Before I could ask Urk how he knew Fazwad was coming, we heard a loud buzz. An instant later, Fazwad himself was standing in front of us.

Fireball poked his head over my shoulder and hissed.

Fazwad was very snooty looking. From the look on his face, he was also very happy. That was a bad sign. "Where is Moongobble?" he demanded.

Just then we heard a big *boom!* from inside the cottage. Urk looked at me and shook his head.

A moment later Moongobble stepped out the door. "Moongobble the Magician, reporting for duty!" he said.

Moongobble is short and roundish. He has merry eyes and a big mustache. Today his robe was stained from magic that had gone bad. The mice who live in his hat were looking over the brim, staring at

Fazwad. One of them made a little spitting noise.

"Ah, there you are, you blithering idiot," said Fazwad with a grin. "You'll be happy to know I have chosen your next Mighty Task." He rubbed his hands together and grinned. "And this one should settle things for good!"

CHAPTER 2

THE SECOND MIGHTY TASK

"What is the task?" asked Moongobble.

I noticed he had a green smudge on his nose, which probably meant some spell had just blown up. I wondered if there was a new piece of cheese in the cottage. When Moongobble's spells went bad, they mostly turned things into cheese. It was not very good magic. But it was usually pretty good cheese.

Fazwad pulled a crystal ball from his sleeve and waved his hand over the top. A mist appeared inside.

As the mist began to clear it showed something big and hairy. I moved closer, to get a better look.

Fireball poked his head over my shoulder so he could see too.

It was a monster.

I looked more closely. The monster's shoulders were shaking, and I realized that it was crying.

"Behold the Weeping Werewolf!" said Fazwad. "Your task, Moongobble, is to bring me a bottle of his tears!"

I swallowed. "Aren't werewolves dangerous?" I asked.

"It wouldn't be a Mighty Task if it weren't dangerous," replied Fazwad with a sneer.

He did not look at me when he said this, even though it was my question he was answering. Fazwad always acted as if I were not there at all.

"Why is he weeping?" asked Moongobble.

"That's not your concern," Fazwad snapped. "All you have to do is bring me those tears." He gave Moongobble one of his nasty smiles. "So . . . do you accept the task? Or shall we call an end to this nonsense right now?" He changed his voice, making it sound almost friendly. "Why not forget about magic, Moongobble? You're just not cut out for it."

"Of course I accept the task," Moongobble said, sounding as close to angry as I had ever heard him. "Where do I find this werewolf?"

Fazwad's friendly look vanished. "You don't think I'm going to make this easy for you, do you? You have to find the werewolf on your own! I'll give you five days to do it."

"Don't be silly," said Urk. "The next full moon isn't for two weeks. Even you can't expect Moongobble to get tears from a werewolf until the moon is full!"

Fazwad laughed. "That's not my problem, is it?

Five days is all you have. I'll be back six days from now to see if you have the tears. And don't try to fool me, Moongobble. I know how to test them to see if they're real."

I knew Moongobble would never try to cheat on a test. I figured the only reason Fazwad thought about something like that is because it is the kind of thing he would do himself.

"Good luck, Moongobble," said Fazwad with a nasty laugh. "You're going to need it!" He sniffed twice. Then he swirled his cape around him and disappeared in a puff of blue smoke.

Even after he was gone, a sour odor lingered in the air.

CHAPTER 3

How to Find a Werewolf

"A werewolf." Moongobble sighed. "What will he think of next?"

"Something nasty, that's for certain," said Fireball.

We went into the cottage, where we sat around Moongobble's table, trying to figure out what to do.

Fireball hooked his feet into the back of my chair and rested his chin on my shoulder. His breath was hot against my cheek.

The mice in Moongobble's hat came back out. They looked angry, and a little frightened.

Urk sat in his usual spot, right on the table. "Well, there are two things we have to do," he said at last.

"What are they?" asked Moongobble.

"First, we must find out where the Weeping Werewolf lives. And second—" He stopped, as if he didn't want to finish the sentence.

"What?" I asked. "Find out where he lives and then what?"

Urk shrugged. "Then we have to find out a way to get some of his tears without getting torn to shreds."

"Let's start by figuring out where he lives," Moongobble said. "It's simpler."

He went to the shelf and started to take down some books. He had to climb on the stool to reach them. Soon he had a pile of books all around him and was sitting on the stool, reading. "Edward, fetch me some silver whistlewort," he called, without looking up.

Silver whistlewort is a plant we gather in the forest. I fetched the bottle from the shelf where we keep it. "Here it is," I said, taking it to Moongobble.

He looked up from his reading. "Here what is?"

he asked. "Oh! The whistlewort. Thank you, Edward."

He took the bottle from me and carried it to the table. Then he took out some of the leaves, mixed them with some other things that he took from his pockets, and made a little pile in the center of the table. Taking his wand from his sleeve, he waved it over the leaves and said, "Iggle! Biggle! Warzza Werewolf!"

Bang! There was a puff of green smoke and a small explosion.

When the smoke cleared, I saw a hole in the center of the table.

"Drat!" said Moongobble. "Here, let me try again."

"I don't think this is going to work," said Urk after Moongobble's third explosion. He wiped a smudge of green soot off his nose. "And if you try that one more time, we're going to need a new table."

"I'm afraid you're right," said Moongobble sadly.

"Now what do we do?" I asked.

"Maybe we should visit Felicity," Urk said.

"Who's Felicity?" asked Fireball.

"A witch," said Urk. "Her professional name is Felicity the Finder. She lives on the far side of the forest."

"I didn't know there was a witch living near Pigbone," I said. The idea made me nervous.

Urk rolled his eyes. "I suspect there is a great deal you do not know, Edward. However, it is no surprise that you would not know about Felicity. She's shy—so shy she would be quite happy if no one even knew she existed. Come on, let's go. It won't take long. We don't need to pack anything more than a lunch, and a gift for Felicity."

"She doesn't mind having visitors?" I asked a little nervously.

"She *hates* it," said Urk.

"She doesn't do anything awful to them, does she?" I asked, trying not to squeak.

"Not if they're polite," he replied.

"And if you're not polite?" asked Fireball, who had a bit of a temper.

Urk shuddered. "You don't want to know."

The mice in Moongobble's hat began to cry.

"Oh, hush!" said Urk, glaring at them. "If you're

quiet—and lucky—Felicity won't even know you're there." He paused, then added, "If you're really lucky, her cat won't notice you either."

The mice scurried through their little door, back into Moongobble's hat.

Urk grinned, looking pleased with himself. "Come on," he said. "Let's get busy."

A few minutes later we headed into the forest.

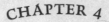

CHAPTER 4

FELICITY

Felicity the Finder lived about two hours' walk from Moongobble's cottage. Her house was hidden under a huge old willow tree, tucked behind the branches as if it were as shy as its owner.

A little brook ran alongside the cottage, and a black cat was sitting out in front when we walked up.

"Hello, Midnight," said Urk, when he saw the cat. "Nice to see you again."

"Nice to see you too, Urk," said the cat, licking a paw.

He didn't sound as if he meant it.

I noticed that Midnight was looking very intently at Moongobble's hat. He couldn't see the mice, though—they had scampered inside the moment they spotted him. He turned his gaze to me. "Is that a dragon on your back?" he asked, sounding fairly surprised for a cat.

"Yes, I'm a dragon!" Fireball said, sticking his head over my shoulder. "Want to make something of it?"

Midnight stared at him for a moment, then said, "Not much to you, is there?"

I grabbed Fireball's nose to keep him from spitting a burst of flame at Midnight. If we wanted Felicity to help us, it wouldn't be a good idea to fry her cat before we went in.

Since we weren't going to toast the kitty, we had some trouble getting past him. Fortunately Urk had suggested that we bring some gifts: cheese for Felicity and a small book of poems about mice for the cat. It took some bargaining, but after a while Midnight said, "All right, you can go in. But let me warn you—when Felicity asks you to leave, you'd better go fast. If she gets too nervous, she can't control herself." He closed his eyes and said happily, "Sometimes things blow up!"

"I understand," said Moongobble, who also tended to blow things up.

Midnight stepped aside and let us in. I glanced over my shoulder as I went through the door. Midnight was leaning against the porch rail, the book of poems open in front of him.

Felicity's cottage was dark inside. A curtain strung across the center of it blocked Felicity from our view. She wouldn't come out to see us, so we had to call our questions through the curtain, and listen very carefully for her answers.

"You want to find the Weeping Werewolf?" she whispered, when we told her what we were after. "Why in the world would you want to do that?"

So we had to explain about Moongobble's mess ups, and Fazwad trying to keep him from joining the society.

Finally Felicity said, "The Weeping Werewolf lives in the Forest of Night. His curse is powerful indeed."

"What do you mean?" asked Moongobble.

"Most men who are werewolves only take wolf form on the night of the full moon. But this man becomes a werewolf every single night."

"Well, that solves one problem," said Urk. "At least we won't have to wait until the next full moon to get those tears."

"What is the safest way to approach him?" asked Moongobble.

"The safest thing is to not get near him at all," said Felicity quickly.

"Well, if we do have to get near him, what should we do?"

"Take plenty of wolf bane, and make sure you've said good-bye to all your loved ones. Now please go. You're making me nervous."

We hurried out the door.

Behind us, I heard something explode.

"I told you," said the cat.

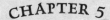

CHAPTER 5

A Visit to a Friend

"This is sounding pretty scary," I said to Moongobble, as we were walking back to the cottage. Urk had hopped off to examine a plant, and Fireball was flying ahead of us, so it was just the two of us talking.

"Maybe we should ask the Rusty Knight to come along," said Moongobble.

The Rusty Knight is a friend of ours who lives on the other side of Pigbone. Since there are only fifteen houses in Pigbone, it's a pretty quick walk to his side of town. When we got back to Moongobble's home we had some lunch, and then set out to visit him.

I noticed that Peter and Thomas did not come out to bother us as we went through town. They might have made fun of Moongobble when he wasn't there, but they didn't say anything when he was with me. Maybe they were afraid he would turn them into cheese.

I like the Rusty Knight's cottage. It is the only place in Pigbone that has real glass in the windows. And he has a very nice garden.

We knocked on the door, and then knocked again. He didn't answer right away. That could mean that he wasn't at home, but what it probably meant was that he didn't hear us. The Rusty Knight's ears do not work very well.

Finally Moongobble cast a spell that made a small explosion.

"Oh, monkey fat," he said. "I didn't mean to do that!"

"That's all right," said Urk. "I suspect that at least he heard it."

Indeed, a moment later the Rusty Knight came

to the door. He had his hand stuck in a vase. "I was cleaning it," he said, holding up his vase-covered hand. "And look what happened!"

"I can get that off for you," said Moongobble. And he was right. It only took three spells and a stick of butter to get the vase off the Rusty Knight's hand. (We used the butter after Moongobble gave up on trying to do it with magic.)

"Well, that's a relief," said the Rusty Knight, once the vase was sitting on the table and he could see his hand again. "I thought I might have to spend the rest of my life that way! Now, how can I help you, Moongobble?"

"We're going on another quest," Moongobble said.

"A brother quest?" said the Rusty Knight. "I didn't know you had a brother."

"*Another* quest," bellowed Urk.

"Ah!" said the Rusty Knight. "I see. And what are you after this time?"

"We need to fetch a bottle of tears from the Weeping Werewolf," Moongobble said.

The Rusty Knight blinked and pulled back from

the table. "Wolf?" he cried. "Where wolf? Here?"

"Werewolf!" bellowed Urk. "As in a man who becomes a wolf when the moon is full. Except this one doesn't wait for a full moon."

The Rusty Knight opened his eyes very wide. "Werewolves are not the kind of thing a knight usually tackles," he said. "We're more in the line of slaying ogres, giants, and dragons."

"Hey," said Fireball. "I resent that!"

"Sorry," said the Rusty Knight. "But you take my point."

"Even so, we would like to have you along," said Moongobble.

The Rusty Knight looked at his hand, then at the vase. "Well, I do owe you a favor," he said. "I guess I had better come along. Do you suppose you could give me a hand with my armor? It's not easy to get into."

Working together, Moongobble, Fireball, and I soon had the Rusty Knight dressed.

"All set to go!" he said happily. Then he asked a question that made me wish we had never come to visit him. "Have you asked Edward's mother if he can go?"

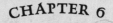

CHAPTER 6

WARNINGS

Our next stop was my own cottage. I knew we really did have to ask Mother. But I was afraid she would say no and I didn't think I could stand it if I didn't get to go along.

At first things did not look good. Mother did not like the idea, any more than she had liked the idea of me going along on Moongobble's first quest.

"But look how well that trip turned out!" I said.

"And now he has me to protect him," added Fireball, sticking his head over my shoulder. "You can't get much better protection than a dragon."

"You're not much of a dragon," Mother said sourly.

Still, after Moongobble, Urk, and the Rusty Knight had all assured Mother that they would keep me out of danger, Mother agreed to let me go. Then she packed some food for all of us. Moongobble had plenty of food of his own but Mother was convinced we would starve if she didn't send some along too.

We all slept at Moongobble's that night, because we wanted to get a very early start. After all, it was a two-day walk to the Forest of Night.

Along the way we stopped to collect wolf bane. Urk was the best at spotting it. He would hop along ahead of us, then shout, "Look over here!"

Soon we had a lot of the stuff.

I wondered if a simple plant could really protect us from a werewolf.

Late on the afternoon of the second day a rabbit hopped up to us and said, "You do know where this road leads, don't you?"

"Of course," said Moongobble. "It goes to the Forest of Night."

"Then what are you doing walking on it?" cried the rabbit, wringing his paws. "Turn back, turn back, while you still can!" Lowering his voice he added, "Many go in, but few come out."

Then he turned and hopped away.

"Wait!" called Moongobble.

But the rabbit was gone.

"That was very strange," said Urk.

"You mean that the rabbit could talk?" I asked.

"No, that he made sense! Rabbits are usually complete idiots. But now that you mention it, the fact that he spoke to us in human words is weird too."

I had gotten used to talking animals; after all, Urk and Fireball were both pretty chatty. But they were magical animals. Most animals couldn't talk that way, not even the mice in Moongobble's hat.

I was still thinking about that when I heard a deep voice say, "The rabbit is right. Turn back while you still can."

I looked up. A huge badger was waddling in our direction. Clearly he was the one who had spoken.

"We can't turn back," Moongobble said. "We've

got a job to do, and we're going to do it."

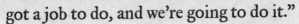

The badger shook his head sadly, then said, "Many go in, but few come out. Oh, well. Don't say I didn't warn you. Ah, there's my burrow." And with that, he dove into a hole in the ground and disappeared.

"Stranger and stranger," Urk said.

We hadn't walked much farther when we met a skunk who stood up in the center of the road, spread his arms, and said, "O foolish wanderers! Turn back while there's still time!"

"We can't turn back," said Moongobble. He was starting to sound cranky now. "We have urgent business in the forest."

I was afraid the skunk was going to spray us. But instead he just said, "More the fools you. Many go in, but few come out."

Then he scampered away.

A few minutes after we met the skunk, the Rusty Knight said, "Look, there's a sign!"

When we got closer, we were able to read it. It said: FOREST OF NIGHT—ONE MILE. MANY GO IN, BUT FEW COME OUT. TURN BACK NOW, WHILE YOU STILL CAN.

We didn't turn back, though. We had a job to do.

Near the edge of the forest we met a man. He was rather strange looking, with a single thick eyebrow that went straight across his face. He seemed alarmed to find us there.

"What are you doing?" he asked. "Where are you going?"

"We're on a quest," Moongobble said. "It takes us into the Forest of Night."

"This is a bad place to be questing," the man said. "It's not safe—especially not for a boy. Especially not now."

"Why not now?" asked Moongobble.

The man looked at the sky and shuddered. "It's only a few hours until nightfall. Strange things happen in that forest at night."

"We have a mission," said Moongobble firmly. Then he turned to me and said, "But maybe you should stay here with this man."

"No!" cried the man. "That is not possible!"

"What was the matter with him?" I asked as we continued on.

"Who knows," said Urk. "Living this close to the Forest of Night would probably make anyone crazy."

A mile later we saw another sign. It said:

YOU ARE NOW ENTERING THE FOREST OF NIGHT—YOU FOOL!

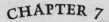

CHAPTER 7

THE FOREST OF NIGHT

It was broad daylight when we walked into the forest. But as soon as we passed the first tree, it seemed that darkness had fallen. Not complete darkness. It was more like the darkness of a night when the moon is almost full.

Moongobble tried to light the way for us. Picking up a stick the size of his arm, he waved his hand over it, saying "Iggle! Biggle! Lettembe Lux!"

The stick made a whooshing sound and flew straight into the air. A moment later we heard it explode above us.

Pieces of cheese pattered down around us.

"That was very exciting," said Urk. "And I'm sure it will delight any mice living here. But it's not going to do us much good."

Moongobble scowled at him and looked around for another branch. Holding it up he cried, "Iggle! Biggle! Makka Stikglo!"

The branch melted in his hand, the wood turning into a sticky goo that ran down his arm.

"You need to work on how you say your *a*'s," muttered Urk.

Finally, on his third try, Moongobble managed to make a branch cast a dim green glow. The light made it a little easier to see, but it also made things look even spookier than before. "I guess that will have to do," he said with a sigh. "It's the best spell I can come up with."

Moongobble made two more torches, one for the Rusty Knight and one for me. Green light flickering around us, we pressed deeper into the woods.

"If it's always dark here, how will we know when it really is night?" I asked after a while.

"Of course I'm a real Knight!" cried the Rusty Knight. He sounded hurt.

I repeated my question, more loudly this time.

"Oh, that's easy!" said the Rusty Knight. "We can use my belly for a clock. I *always* know when it's supper time."

We walked on. In the green glow of our torches I could see eyes peering at us from behind trees. Just when I was getting so tired that I didn't think I could go another step, the Rusty Knight said, "My stomach has spoken. It's supper time."

"Before we eat, we must set our trap," Moongobble said.

We found a slender tree and bent it to the ground, then staked it into place. Attached to the tree was a rope. We put a coil of the rope on the ground and covered it with leaves. In the center of the rope we put a big hunk of cheese. (We had planned to use raw meat, but Moongobble got the spell wrong.)

Just as we were finishing, a bloodcurdling howl split the darkness. The sound seemed to crawl up and down my spine. I felt a shiver of terror. Yet at the same time, I felt very sad.

"Well," said Urk softly. "There it is—the howl of the Weeping Werewolf. He must be nearby."

I shivered and peered into the darkness.

I wondered how close the werewolf really was.

I wondered if our trap would work.

Most of all, I wondered what would happen if it didn't.

CHAPTER 8

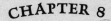

WEREWOLF TRAP

We moved a good distance from the trap. When we had found a place to camp, Fireball started our campfire.

Before Fireball came to live with us, Moongobble had always tried to start our campfires with magic. This never worked quite the way it should. Sometimes the logs turned into cheese—tasty, but not very useful for light and heat. Sometimes the logs screamed and ran away—exciting, but still not very useful. Once, they sprouted roots and turned into a miniature forest. All in all, it was better to

have Fireball do this kind of thing.

"Maybe *you* should make the torches tomorrow," I said to him, once the fire was blazing away.

"Not a good idea," he said, resting his scaly head on my knee. "Real fire is fine for a campsite. But walking through a forest with blazing torches is just asking for trouble. Magical light is safer—even if it is green!"

We arranged ourselves in a circle, with our backs to the flames, so we could watch for any sign of the werewolf. Moongobble, the Rusty Knight, and I were clutching bundles of wolf bane.

"Do you really think this stuff will work?" I asked Fireball.

He yawned, letting out a little puff of smoke. "If it doesn't, I'll just scorch his butt for you," he said.

"Why don't we sing a little campfire song?" asked the Rusty Knight after a while. "I know some good ones. They're a bit naughty, but—"

"For heaven's sake, be quiet," said Urk impatiently.

Suddenly we heard a noise in the bushes, just past the edge of our firelight. "What are you doing here?" growled a harsh voice.

Scary as the voice was, it was also sorrowful—so sad I almost broke out sobbing myself.

Moongobble stood up. "We want to talk to the Weeping Werewolf!" he said.

"Go away!" cried the voice. "Go away while you still can!" Then it burst into tears.

Soon it was blubbering so loudly that it sounded like its heart had broken.

"Go away!" it cried again. Then it turned and rushed off.

"Wait!" Moongobble cried.

To my horror, he ran after the werewolf.

A moment later we heard a howl of surprise, followed by a crashing sound and then yips of anger.

Our trap had worked!

Clutching our torches and our wolf bane, we hurried toward the sounds.

Sure enough, we had caught the werewolf. He was shaped like a man, but he was covered with fur, and had big, pointy ears. He was dangling upside down from the tree, twisting and lurching in a wild attempt to get free from our trap. His eyes were blazing. Terrible snarls came from his mouth.

Moongobble held the bottle under the werewolf's eyes to collect the tears. But the werewolf wasn't crying anymore. All his sorrow had turned to anger. He raged and snapped and howled. But he didn't cry.

Moongobble groaned. "*Now* what do we do?"

CHAPTER 9

How to Make a Werewolf Weep

For a moment we all just stood there. Then I remembered how Thomas and Peter had made me cry a few days ago.

Could that kind of thing work with a werewolf? I figured it couldn't hurt to try. So I decided to ask some questions.

"Hey, werewolf!" I said, trying to sound mean. "Where did you come from?"

He glared at me. But he also started to sniffle.

"How did you get this way, anyway?"

More sniffling.

"Don't you have a family?" I taunted.

At these words he let out a howl of deep sorrow. I felt like a beast myself. I could have asked those questions nicely. But I didn't. I was asking them in a mean way, to make him sad, to make him cry. It was cruel. But we had to get those tears!

"Where is your family, anyway? What happened to them? Did they run away because you're so ugly?"

A horrible sob burst from the werewolf's mouth. A moment later tears poured down his furry cheeks. He wasn't twisting and turning now, just hanging upside down and sobbing.

"Well done," said Moongobble softly. He took the bottle out of his pack and lifted it to the werewolf's cheeks. The tears slid down the werewolf's muzzle, dripping into the bottle.

The sound of his weeping was horrible. It seemed to take forever for his tears to fill the bottle.

At last Moongobble cried, "Got it!" He pulled the bottle away, then pushed a cork into its neck to keep the tears safe. "You can stop crying now," he said to the werewolf.

But sometimes it's easier to start someone crying

than it is to stop them. The werewolf sobbed, and sobbed, and sobbed.

It made me want to cry too.

"I wonder if he'll turn back into a human when morning comes," I said. I spoke the words softly to Fireball. Even so, they only made the werewolf cry harder.

"How will we even know it's morning?" Urk asked gloomily. "It never gets light here in the Forest of Night."

"When my stomach tells me it's time for breakfast, that will mean it's morning," said the Rusty Knight.

I looked at the werewolf. "It doesn't seem right to leave him there till morning," I said.

"Well we can't untie him," said Urk. "There's no telling what he might do!"

The werewolf sobbed even harder.

"Let me try a calming spell," said Moongobble. He rolled up his sleeves and began to wave his wand. "Iggle! Biggle! Hart Zateeze!"

Bang! A puff of green smoke surrounded the werewolf. Then I heard a clunking sound. The werewolf had fallen to the ground. Only he wasn't a werewolf anymore. He was a big hunk of cheese.

Hairy cheese, which was sort of disgusting.

"Dad rat monkey fat!" said Moongobble, shaking his wand. "That wasn't supposed to happen!"

"Well, it did," said Urk with a sigh. "Now we'll have to take turns staying awake in case he starts to change back into himself—his werewolf self."

"Well, it's my fault," Moongobble said. "I'll take the first turn."

I looked at the cheese. I thought I saw some water at one corner.

Was it possible for cheese to weep?

Moongobble had turned me into cheese once, so I knew it didn't hurt, even if it was a little scary. I was still feeling bad about making the werewolf cry. But I was also really tired. After a while I drifted off, falling into a dream of werewolves and witches, green glows and talking toads.

The next thing I knew, the Rusty Knight was saying, "Well, it's morning!"

"It certainly is," said a soft, sad voice.

I shook my head and realized I had been sleeping. Whose voice was that?

I looked up. Sitting beside Moongobble was a very unhappy-looking man. It was the same man we had met at the edge of the forest, the one who had warned us not to go in.

"*You're* the Weeping Werewolf!" I cried. "Why did you tell us to turn back? Were you afraid you would tear us limb from limb?"

"Of course not!" he said, sounding shocked. "I was afraid I would be embarrassed if you caught me sobbing. Which I am. Embarrassed, that is. I had no idea you were going to trap me like this. I don't think it was very nice of you."

The man sounded so sad that I started to think Fazwad had given Moongobble the wrong task. A really good magician would not be worried about collecting a flask of tears.

A really good magician would try to cure the Weeping Werewolf.

CHAPTER 10

WHY THE WEREWOLF WEEPS

"I'm sorry I made you cry last night," I said. "It's just that we had to get those tears. But I really did wonder about the things I asked you. Why are you so sad?"

"Wouldn't you be sad if you were a werewolf and could never see your home and family again?" he asked.

"I suppose I would," said Moongobble. "Even so, you seem sadder than the average werewolf. Not that I've met that many of them. But, well—they do call *you* 'The Weeping Werewolf.' So it would seem that you're sadder than most!"

"I don't know what it's like for other werewolves. All I know is that I miss my wife and child. I don't want to be a werewolf anymore!"

"How did you get to be a werewolf to begin with?" I asked.

The man sat down. "I used to live in a little town called Pigbone-East-of-the-Mountains."

"That's where we live!" I cried.

"Wonderful place, isn't it?" the man said sadly.

I wasn't sure I completely agreed, but I didn't say that just then.

"Anyway," he continued, "one day I set out to go to the market in the big city. My wife warned me not to go. She said there was no reason to leave Pigbone. But we were short on money, and I hoped to sell some of my carvings in the city. Alas, I never got there. Though I knew I should walk around the Forest of Night, I foolishly decided to go straight through it. As I was making my way through the darkness I met an old woman who asked me for a crust of bread."

"You gave it to her, didn't you?" I asked.

"I would have," said the man, "only I didn't have any. That's how poor we were. When I told the old woman I had no bread, she got so angry she cast a spell on me. That's when I became the weeping werewolf. I haven't seen home or family since."

"Is there any way to cure you?" Urk asked.

The man sighed. "When the woman cursed me, she said,

'Werewolf, werewolf you shall be
And no more see the light,
Until the day the sun shines
In the Forest of the Night.'"

"What the heck does that mean?" I asked.

"It's a riddle of some sort," Moongobble said. "They're very common in magic. But I can't make any sense of it."

"I suppose if we chopped down enough trees, the sun would shine here," said the Rusty Knight, once we had repeated the riddle loudly enough for him to understand it.

"I wouldn't do that," said the man. "It's very dangerous to chop down a tree in this forest." He sighed. "If I only became a wolf on full-moon nights I might have been able to go home, and escape back here once a month. But Pigbone is two days away, so I can't get there without turning into a wolf. And who knows what terrible thing I might do then? At least here in the Forest of Night I can't harm anyone."

"Why can't you harm anyone here?" I asked.

"Because there's no one here to harm!" he replied. "Except for the old woman. She lives here."

"In a cottage?" I asked.

"In a cave," said the man. "But I don't dare go near it. Once was bad enough! Who knows what she might do to me next time."

"We will go and talk to her," said Moongobble.

"We will?" I asked.

"Of course," said Moongobble. "It is the least we can do in return for the tears this man has given us."

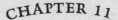

CHAPTER 11

SHINING!

We stood in front of the cave. Snakes hung down in front of it, like a curtain. Well, they would have been like a curtain if they hadn't kept hissing and moving.

"This is not good," said Urk. "Snakes like to eat toads."

"Leave this one to me," said Fireball. He flew off my shoulder and landed in front of the cave. I thought he might be going to blast the snakes with flames. I wasn't sure that was a good idea. It would get rid of the snakes, but it might make the old lady really mad. But I was wrong. What came out of his mouth wasn't fire. It was a lot of hissing sounds. The snakes twisted and squirmed. Then they pulled sideways to make an opening.

"Distant cousins," said Fireball, when he flew back to me. "You just have to know how to talk to them. Hurry up, before they forget what I asked them to do. They're not very bright."

Clutching our green torches, we hurried into the cave. The first part was like a hallway made of stone. After about ten feet it opened into a big room. In the center of the room was a fire. A big black kettle hung over the fire, bubbling and steaming.

Sitting beside the fire, rocking in a chair, was a beautiful woman.

I was so surprised that I forgot Moongobble was supposed to do the talking. "Who are you?" I asked.

"Who do you want me to be?" she replied, in a voice as beautiful as her face.

"We were looking for the old woman," I said.

"I can be an old woman," she answered. Before I could even blink, the beautiful young woman was gone. In her place sat an old hag. "How's that?" she

asked in a creaky voice. "Better?"

"This is very weird," whispered Fireball. His breath was warm against my ear.

"You're a very strange group," said the old woman, tugging at her chin. "A magician, a knight, a toad, a dragon, a boy, and . . . ah, the man who had no bread for me! I wondered when you would show up here. Have you brought me some bread at last?"

The woman reminded me of Peter and Thomas. She was being mean just for the sake of being mean.

"He has no bread!" I said angrily. "And you were mean to punish him when he didn't have it before! You've got no reason to act like that!"

The old woman looked at me in astonishment.

At the same moment the werewolf-man cried out, "I feel . . . strange!"

"So," whispered the old woman. "It's happened at last. The son shines in the Forest of Night."

"What are you talking about?" I asked.

The old woman didn't answer. Instead, she vanished, and her fire with her. Our torches went out too. That should have left us in complete darkness. But it didn't. The cave was still lit by a soft glow.

Only I couldn't figure out where it was coming from.

"Edward!" said Moongobble, sounding astonished. "You . . . you're shining!"

"I am?" I said, putting my hands to my face.

"Edward?" asked the werewolf-man. "Is your name really Edward?"

"Of course," I said, feeling confused, and a little afraid.

The man put out his arms.

"Edward from Pigbone," he cried. "I am your father!"

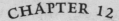

CHAPTER 12

No Tears, No Magic

By the time we left the cave, I had stopped glowing—which was sort of a relief.

It was Urk who explained it all. "You didn't quite understand the curse," he told my father. "You didn't need the sun to shine in the Forest of Night to be cured. You needed your *own* son to shine—which Edward did by standing up to the old woman. It was a shining deed, and it broke the spell."

My own father was standing with his arm around me. It felt good but it also felt strange. I was not used to having a father!

"You were only a baby when I left," he kept saying. "Only a baby."

"Come on," said Urk, after a little while. "You can talk it over later. We should get out of this forest before something else happens!"

But something else did happen. We had barely left the Forest of Night when a man came stumbling toward us. His face was as sad as my father's had been when he was the Weeping Werewolf.

"What's wrong?" Moongobble asked, as the man drew near.

The man burst into tears.

"Sheesh," muttered Urk. "They ought to change the name of this place from the 'Forest of Night' to the 'Forest of Weeping and Wailing.'"

"It's my daughter!" sobbed the man. "My daughter has been turned to stone by an evil spell!"

"Perhaps I can help," said Moongobble, pushing up his sleeves. "I am a magician!"

"There's only one way to save her," said the man, wiping at his tears. "That's why I'm heading—" He gulped and pointed toward the forest. "That's why I'm heading there. The only way to free my daughter from her curse is to pour a bottle of tears from the Weeping Werewolf over her head. Then she will turn back into a real girl." He stared at the forest in horror. "I may not live through it but I have to get those tears!"

"Who cast this spell?" asked Urk.

"The old woman of the woods," said the man, wiping at his tears.

"Just as I suspected," Urk muttered. "She is angry because we broke the other spell, and this is her way of getting back at us!"

I got a sinking feeling in the pit of my stomach. I knew what Moongobble would do—and he did it. Reaching into his robe, he pulled out the bottle of tears. "There is no Weeping Werewolf anymore," he said sadly. "But I have a bottle of his tears. Here it is. They should bring your daughter back to life."

"How can I ever thank you?" cried the man, clasping the bottle in astonishment. "How can I possibly repay you?"

"Be a good father," said Moongobble, his voice soft and sad.

The man raced off, shouting with happiness.

"Well, that's done it," grumbled Urk. "Now you'll never be a magician!"

"Would you have wanted me to do anything different?" asked Moongobble.

"Of course not!" said the toad gruffly. "You did the right thing. It's just very annoying!"

"I could try to cry some more, if that would help," said Father.

"Won't make any difference now that you're human again," said Urk gruffly.

We were quiet as we walked back to the cottage. I wondered if Fazwad would really make Moongobble stop doing magic, even though he had given up the tears to do a good deed. It just didn't seem right. On the other hand, Fazwad seemed to care more about rules than he did about right and wrong. And even I knew that Moongobble wasn't a very good magician. But somehow he always managed to *do* good, even while he was messing up.

Mother claims it is because he has such a good heart.

Shouldn't that count for something?

No one said much as we reached the garden behind the cottage. We were all worried about Moongobble, and trying to think of what to say when Fazwad showed up. Only I was having a hard time thinking about that, because I was also excited, and confused, about having found my father. I was a little shy about it too. What was he like? What would it be like to have him home with us again? What would Mother think?

"Excuse me," said Urk. "I need to check something inside." He hopped through the cottage door, looking like a bran muffin on springs.

The rest of us stayed outside. "I'm nervous about going home," said Father, looking down the hill. "I've been gone for so long. What will your mother say when she sees me?"

Before I could answer we heard a snap. An instant later Fazwad appeared, surrounded by his usual cloud of blue smoke.

"Well, Moongobble," he said, smiling in a sickening way. "Do you have those tears?"

Moongobble spread his hands. "I had them," he said sadly. "But they're gone."

Fazwad laughed. "Do you expect me to believe that? 'I had them, but they're gone.' Really, Moongobble, if you're going to invent an excuse you should do better than that. Ah, well. It doesn't make any difference. You've failed the test, and it's all over. You can stop trying to be a magician now and leave the rest of us alone." He held out his hand. "You might as well give me your wand and be done with it."

Shoulders drooping, Moongobble stepped forward. He reached into his robe for the wand.

"Wait!" said Father. "It's my fault he doesn't have the tears."

"It doesn't make any difference whose fault it is!" snapped Fazwad. "Moongobble is finished!"

"Not so fast, Fazwad," said a voice from the cottage door, "This isn't over yet!"

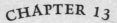

CHAPTER 13

URK HOPS IN

It was Urk. He was smiling.

Fazwad glared at him. "What are you talking about, you interfering toad?"

Urk hopped closer. "Your test was unfair," he scolded, shaking a finger at Fazwad. "Moongobble *can't* get tears from the Weeping Werewolf, because there *is* no Weeping Werewolf!"

"Nonsense!" said Fazwad. "Of course there's a Weeping Werewolf!"

"Prove it," said Urk.

Fazwad pulled the crystal ball from the pocket of his robe.

At the same time Moongobble scooped up Urk and put him on his shoulder.

Holding the clear sphere in one hand, Fazwad waved the other hand over it, muttering strange words. But no matter how hard he tried, he could not call up an image of the Weeping Werewolf.

"Drat you, Moongobble!" he cried. "I don't know what you've done, but I know you had something to do with this. The test is void." He took a deep breath. Then he smiled, which was a bad sign. "I guess you'll just have to do something *else* for your second Mighty Task."

"I don't think so," said Urk smoothly. "Have you read the handbook lately?"

He meant the *Society of Magicians Handbook*, of course.

Fazwad glared at him.

"Page forty-seven," added Urk helpfully.

Fazwad snapped his fingers. With a small puff of blue smoke, a book appeared in his hand. He flipped to page forty-seven, stared at it for a moment, then began to sputter angrily.

"I'll recite it for you, if you don't want to read it out loud," said Urk, sounding a trifle smug. "'If a Mighty Task turns out to be invalid, then the candidate'—meaning Moongobble in this case—'shall receive credit for it as if he had passed it.'"

"You interfering toad!" cried Fazwad. He stopped and took a deep breath, as if it were beneath his dignity to lose his temper. Then he put his hands together and smiled a thin, nasty smile. "Don't worry, Moongobble. I'll be back soon with your third test. And this one will be a real showstopper!"

He sniffed twice, swirled his cape around him, and disappeared in a big puff of blue smoke.

The mice rushed to the edge of Moongobble's hat. They shook their little fists and made rude noises.

"I do not like that man," said Urk.

"Now, now," said Moongobble. "There's a little bit of good in everyone. All we have to do is find it."

"Finding the good in Fazwad is going to take some powerful magic," muttered Fireball.

We heard a noise. It was Mother. She had climbed halfway up the hill and was ringing a bell to summon us for supper.

"Aha!" said the Rusty Knight. "I knew it was time for supper! My stomach never lies!"

I took my father by the hand. "Come on," I said. "Let's go home. Mother is waiting for us."

"And boy is she in for a surprise," Urk said.

Father and I started down the hill.

All our friends came with us.

I was happy, and nervous, and more excited than I had ever been. I had known my life was going to change when Moongobble came to town.

I just had never known how much!

About the Author and Illustrator

BRUCE COVILLE is the author of nearly ninety books for young readers, including the international best-seller *My Teacher Is an Alien*. He has been a teacher, a toymaker, a cookware salesman, and a grave digger. In addition to his work as an author, Bruce is much in demand as a speaker and as a storyteller. He is also the founder and president of Full Cast Audio, a company dedicated to producing unabridged recordings of children's books in a full-cast format. For more information about Bruce check out www.brucecoville.com.

KATHERINE COVILLE is an artist, sculptor, and doll maker who specializes in highly detailed images of creatures never before seen in this world. She has illustrated several books written by her husband, Bruce Coville, including *Goblins in the Castle, Aliens Ate My Homework,* and the Space Brat series.

Bruce and Katherine live in Syracuse, New York, with a varying assortment of pets and children.